Pretty Poodle Parlour

Pretty Poodle Parlour

Written by **Angela McAllister**

Illustrated by **Diane Ewen**

Orion
Children's Books

ORION CHILDREN'S BOOKS

First published in Great Britain in 2016
by Hodder and Stoughton

1 3 5 7 9 10 8 6 4 2

Text © Angela McAllister, 2016
Illustrations © Diane Ewen, 2016

The moral rights of the author and illustrator have been asserted.

A CIP catalogue record for this book
is available from the British Library.

ISBN 978 1 4440 1610 9

Printed and bound in China

The paper and board used in this book are from well-managed forests
and other responsible sources.

MIX
Paper from
responsible sources
FSC® C104740

Orion Children's Books
An imprint of
Hachette Children's Group
Part of Hodder and Stoughton
Carmelite House
50 Victoria Embankment
London EC4Y 0DZ

An Hachette UK Company
www.hachette.co.uk

www.orionchildrensbooks.co.uk

For Georgina

Contents

Chapter 1

This is Mimi. She loves to make
everyone happy.

Every day, she goes to Pretty Poodle Parlour, to help Madame Shampoodle.

Sometimes she gives the customers
a cup of tea,

or a shampoo,

sometimes a haircut

or a fluffy blow dry.

She knows that the Valentino twins
like different bows.

She knows that Bonzo Bulldog
is ticklish behind
his ears.

She knows that Truffle Truelove won't take her collar off because it has real diamonds.

And she knows that the Wriggly
pups won't sit still to wait until
somebody sings 'The tail on the dog
goes wag, wag, wag!'

'Clever girl, Mimi,' says Madame.
'You always make the customers
happy.'

Chapter 2

One morning, Mimi found Madame
Shampoodle reading a fashion
magazine.

'I'm trying to choose a 'Style of the Month' for our window display,' said Madame.
'What about curls?' asked Mimi.
'We've already had curls,' said Madame.

'Topknots?' said Mimi.
Madame shook her head. 'It's got
to be amazing, Mimi. Something
everyone will notice.'

At that moment, a shy poodle
stepped into the salon.
'It's my niece Florence,' said
Madame. 'She has come to help in
the salon.'

Florence smiled and Mimi liked her
at once.
'Will you show me what to do?'
said Florence.
'Of course,' said Mimi.

'You can help us choose a 'Style
of the Month', Florence,' said
Madame.

'If we aren't too busy, I want to change these old yellow curtains and give the salon a fresh new look,' said Madame.
'That sounds fun,' said Florence.

Chapter 3

The first customer was Barkley
Sheepdog.
Snip, snip, snip! Madame
Shampoodle trimmed his eyebrows
so he could see properly again.

Next came Patch, who'd been for a muddy walk.

Mimi ran him a bubble bath.
'Ooh la la!' said Madame. 'I'll need all my skill to make you handsome again!'

Mimi and Florence washed,
brushed and blow dried.
They were soon so busy that
nobody had time to think about the
curtains.

They were so busy that nobody noticed a big black car park outside. A mysterious dog walked into the salon.
Everybody stopped and stared.

'Gloria Greyhound is making a film nearby today,' he said, 'but her hairdresser is ill. Can you help, Madame?'

Madame Shampoodle put down
her scissors.
'Gloria Greyhound - the most
famous film star in the country?'
'Yes,' he said.

'Well, I am happy to help,' said
Madame, 'but who would look
after the salon?'
 'I can do it,' said Mimi. 'I know
what the customers want.'
'Thank you, Mimi,' said Madame.

'We can do it together,' said Florence. 'Mimi will show me what to do.'

'Wonderful!' cried Madame Shampoodle. 'I know I can rely on you both.'

Chapter 4

Mimi and Florence had to
work hard without Madame
Shampoodle.

Florence fetched clean towels while Mimi cut hair.

Then Florence painted nails while Mimi blow dried.

Then Florence tied bows while
Mimi trimmed whiskers and paws.

At last the salon was empty.

'Let's have a tea break,' said Mimi.

Before they could put the kettle on,
Truffle Truelove arrived.

'I've come for a new colour, Mimi
darling,' said Truffle. 'Where is
Madame Shampoodle?'

'She's gone to help Gloria
Greyhound, the famous film star,'
said Mimi. 'I can do the colour
for you.'
'Thank you,' said Truffle. 'I'm
going to shut my eyes for a nap.
Don't wake me until it's done.'

Mimi was about to fetch Truffle's colour dye, when Basil Wriggly and his pups tumbled in. 'Can you trim their nails, Mimi?' said Basil. 'I'll be back in an hour.'

And he hurried off.

The Wriggly pups chased each
other around the salon.
'I'll trim their nails,' said Florence,
trying to grab their collars, 'but
how do I get them to sit still?'

'Can you sing 'The tail on the dog goes wag, wag, wag?' asked Mimi.
Florence shook her head.
'Then I'd better look after the puppies,' said Mimi. 'You can do Truffle's colour.'

'There should be a bowl of colour dye in the back room. Brush it on carefully all over.'

'Don't worry, Mimi,' said Florence. 'I'll be careful.'

The Wriggly pups were so excited
that Mimi had to sing to them six
times.

When at last they left, Mimi went
to help Florence.

But Florence had just finished
and...

Oh NO!

Chapter 5

'You've dyed Truffle blue!'
whispered Mimi.
Florence looked worried. 'Isn't that
what she wanted?'

'She usually has pink,' said Mimi.
I've never seen any customers
coloured blue before. Where did
you get that dye?'
'It was in the back room,' said
Florence and she began to cry.

Truffle Truelove opened her eyes.
'What's the matter?' she said. 'Why
are you upset?'

Then she saw her paws.
'I'm blue!' she cried in horror.

'Oh dear,' said Florence. 'I've made
a terrible mistake.'

Mimi hurried into the back room and found the bowl of pink dye. 'What was the blue for?' asked Florence.

Mimi remembered that Madame
wanted to give the salon a fresh
new look.

'That blue dye must be for the
curtains!' she said.

Chapter 6

Everyone felt bad.
Truffle felt bad because she was
blue.

Florence felt bad because she'd
made a terrible mistake.

And Mimi felt bad because she'd promised Madame that she would keep the customers happy.

'You could wear a coat and hat,'
said Florence.
'It's far too hot,' said Truffle.

'You could stay indoors until it
grows out?' said Florence.
'I like to go shopping,' said Truffle.

'You could wear a disguise,' said
Florence.
'Everyone will still notice me,' said
Truffle and a big teardrop trickled
down her blue face.

Suddenly Mimi had an idea.

She fetched Madame Shampoodle's
camera.
'Can I take your photo, Truffle?'
asked Mimi.
'But I'm all blue!' said Truffle.

'Exactly,' said Mimi. 'Madame has been searching for an amazing new style that people will notice. Why don't we make blue our 'Style of the Month'?'

Truffle dried her tears. 'It is a very pretty shade,' she said.

'We could call it 'Truffle Blue!' said Mimi.

Truffle beamed proudly.

'My very own colour!' she said.

'Yes, I'd love to be the 'Style of the Month'.'

Chapter 7

When Madame Shampoodle
returned that afternoon she got
a surprise. In the window was a
poster of Truffle Truelove - blue
all over!

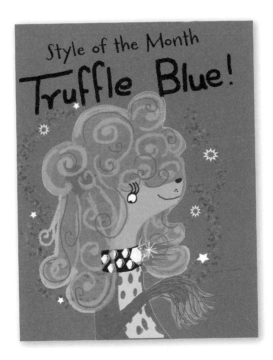

'I hope she likes it,' Florence whispered to Mimi.
Madame smiled.
'Clever girls!' she said. 'I see we'll have to choose another colour for the curtains!'

While Florence was telling
Madame what had happened,
the salon door opened and in
walked Gloria Greyhound.
'I saw your window on my way
home, Madame,' she said. 'What a
beautiful colour! When my film is
finished I'd like a 'Truffle Blue' tail.'

'Ooh la la!' said Madame
Shampoodle. 'Our salon will
be famous!'
'Thank you for putting everything
right, Mimi,' said Florence. Mimi
gave her a hug. 'I love to make
everyone happy!' she said.